GEO

FRIENDS
OF ACPL

P9-DYP-157

LET'S WORK IT OUT™

How to deal with TEASING

Julie Fiedler

PowerKiDS
press

New York

Published in 2007 by The Rosen Publishing Group, Inc.
29 East 21st Street, New York, NY 10010

First Edition

Editor: Jennifer Way
Book Design: Ginny Chu
Layout Design: Kate Laczynski

Photo Credits: Cover, pp. 1, 16 © Denis Boissavy/Getty Images; pp. 4, 8, 10 © Corbis; pp. 6, 12, 14, 18, 20 © Shutterstock.

Library of Congress Cataloging-in-Publication Data

Fieldler, Julie.
  How to deal with teasing / Julie Fiedler. — 1st ed.
      p. cm. — (Let's work it out)
  Includes index.
  ISBN-13: 978-1-4042-3675-2 (lib. bdg.)
  ISBN-10: 1-4042-3675-9 (lib. bdg.)
  1. Teasing—Juvenile literature. I. Title. II. Series.

  BF637.T43F54 2007
  302.3—dc22

                                          2006030146

Manufactured in the United States of America

Contents

Teasing can be playful talk between people. If it goes too far, teasing can cause hurt feelings.

What Is Teasing?

You might have heard teasing words as a joke, such as "squirt," "four eyes," or "Einstein." Teasing is meant to be playful. Most of the time people tease friends, **siblings**, or fellow students.

When teasing is friendly and playful, everyone will laugh and have fun. Sometimes teasing can be taken too far and people's feelings get hurt. By understanding the difference between playful teasing and hurtful teasing, you can help keep things fun for everyone.

People can be sensitive about being teased about certain things, such as wearing glasses.

Going Too Far

You can tell the difference between playful teasing and hurtful teasing by looking at how the person being teased **reacts**. If he or she is laughing and joking along with the person doing the teasing, then it is OK.

If the person being teased does not laugh, looks sad, or becomes angry, then the teasing has gone too far. It is time to stop it. A person might be **sensitive** about something, such as having glasses. Calling that person four eyes might hurt his or her feelings, even if other teases do not.

A person who is being teased can feel very alone.
Over time teasing can cause a person to develop low self-esteem.

When Teasing Hurts

When teasing goes too far or when it happens too often, it can become hurtful. The person being teased can get hurt feelings or become angry. He or she may not want to play with the teaser anymore. He or she may even want to stop going to school as a way to **avoid** the teaser.

If someone is teased a lot, he or she can **develop** low **self-esteem**. If a person continues teasing someone even when he or she knows it hurts that person, it is known as bullying. It is important to learn to deal with teasing.

A person who is teased on the school bus might start to hate riding it or want to avoid riding it.

Everyone Gets Teased

Teasing is a fact of life. Almost everyone gets teased at one time or another. Tall kids get teased and so do short kids. Even adults tease each other sometimes. Teasing can happen anywhere, such as in school, around your neighborhood, or on the school bus.

If you are being teased, know that you are not alone even if you feel that you are. If teasing bothers you, then it can help to understand why people tease each other.

People may tease someone they have a crush on, or like, because they find it hard to say how they feel. This kind of teasing can be playful, but it can also be mean.

Why People Tease

People often tease to get attention. If they have low self-esteem, they might hope that teasing will make them feel powerful. Other people may tease because they do not know how to show their feelings. They might tease someone they have a crush on.

Sometimes people tease others for being different from them. Lots of times people see others teasing and **imitate** them. These people feel like they are part of a group, even though it means being part of a group that is doing something wrong.

Sometimes a group of people may tease one person.
The group of teasers is being influenced by peer presure.

Peer Pressure

When a group of people **influences** someone to take part in something, it is called **peer pressure**. Peer pressure can be either good or bad. If a well-liked person teases someone, others may want to do it too. They might think it will help them fit in or they might even be afraid of being teased themselves.

If you think teasing is hurting someone's feelings, you do not have to join in. It is not cool to hurt other people's feelings.

If you feel hurt by someone's teasing, it is important to tell him so that he will know he should stop.

What If You Are Being Teased?

If you are being teased, your feelings will tell you whether it is playful or hurtful. If teasing bothers you and you are friends with the teaser, tell him or her how the teasing makes you feel. Others may not know when teasing has crossed the line into being hurtful. Telling them can help them know when to stop.

If the teaser is not a friend, you might first try to **ignore** the teasing and walk away, or turn it around into a joke. If the teasing does not stop, you should ask a trusted adult for help.

If you are teasing people and hurting their feelings,
you should try to understand why you are doing it.

What If You Are Teasing Others?

If you have ever teased others, think about why you did it. Were they different from you? Were you afraid of them? Maybe you felt peer pressure to take part in teasing someone. If you tease people a lot, they may avoid you. You could even lose friends.

If you want to tease others, think about how you would feel if you were being teased. Understanding what someone else is going through can help you learn to treat others with respect.

Talking to a trusted adult is a good way to work through your feelings and get help with your problems.

Talking About It

If teasing bothers you, talk to a parent or trusted adult. Talking can help if you are the person being teased or the person teasing others. If you are being teased, talk about what happened and how it made you feel.

If you think you are teasing others too much, talk to an adult to help you learn how to stop. If teasing ever turns into bullying, tell an adult right away. It is never OK for people to hurt each other on purpose.

Dealing with Teasing

It is important to understand the difference between playful teasing and mean teasing. Always be **aware** of how people react to teasing. Remember that the person being teased controls how far the teasing goes. If no one is laughing, then it is time to stop.

It is not OK to hurt other people's feelings. If you have hurt someone's feelings, it is important to **apologize**. An apology can help a person begin to feel better. Talk about your feelings and practice the different ways you have just learned to deal with teasing and being teased.

Glossary

apologize (uh-PAH-leh-jyz) To tell someone you are sorry.

avoid (uh-VOYD) To stay away from something.

aware (uh-WER) Knowing what is going on around you.

develop (dih-VEH-lup) To grow.

ignore (ig-NOR) To pay no attention to something.

imitate (IH-muh-tayt) To do something like someone else.

influences (IN-floo-ens-ez) Gets others to do something.

peer pressure (PEER PREH-shur) When friends or classmates make you feel like you have to do something you do not want to do.

reacts (ree-AKTS) Acts because something has happened.

self-esteem (self-uh-STEEM) Happiness with oneself.

sensitive (SEN-sih-tiv) Easily hurt.

siblings (SIH-blingz) People's sisters or brothers.

Index

A
adult(s), 11, 17, 21
apology, 22
attention, 13

B
bullying, 9, 21

F
feelings, 5, 9, 13,
 15, 17, 22
friend(s), 5, 17, 19

G
glasses, 7
group, 13, 15

J
joke, 5, 17

P
parent, 21
peer pressure, 15,
 19

R
respect, 19

S
school, 9, 11
self-esteem, 9, 13
siblings, 5
students, 5

W
words, 5

Web Sites

Due to the changing nature of Internet links, PowerKids Press has developed an online list of Web sites related to the subject of this book. This site is updated regularly. Please use this link to access the list:
www.powerkidslinks.com/lwio/teasing/